LOUDMOUTH George
and the Sixth-Grade Bully

LOUDMOUTH George
and the Sixth-Grade Bully

Nancy Carlson

PUFFIN BOOKS

for Lloyd, who has survived the bullies
of the world

PUFFIN BOOKS

Viking Penguin Inc., 40 West 23rd Street, New York, New York 10010, U.S.A.
Penguin Books Ltd, 27 Wrights Lane, London W8 5TZ (Publishing & Editorial) and
Harmondsworth, Middlesex, England (Distribution & Warehouse)
Penguin Books Australia Ltd, Ringwood, Victoria, Australia
Penguin Books Canada Limited, 2801 John Street, Markham, Ontario, Canada L3R 1B4
Penguin Books (N.Z.) Ltd, 182–190 Wairau Road, Auckland 10, New Zealand

First published by Carolrhoda Books, Inc. 1983
Published in Picture Puffins 1985
5 7 9 10 8 6
Copyright © Nancy Carlson, 1983
All rights reserved

Library of Congress Cataloging in Publication Data
Carlson, Nancy L.   Loudmouth George and the sixth-grade bully.
Summary: After having his lunch repeatedly stolen
by a bully twice his size, Loudmouth George and his
friend Harriet teach him a lesson he'll never forget.
1. Children's stories, American.   [1. Bullies—
Fiction. 2. Rabbits—Fiction.] I. Title.
PZ7.C21665Lq 1985   [E]   84-18120 ISBN 0-14-050510-5

Manufactured in the U.S.A.

It was the first day of school. George was excited.

Suddenly an enormous sixth grader jumped out of the bushes. George had never seen him before, but he knew right away that this must be Big Mike, the new kid in town.

"Hi-ya, squirt," said Big Mike. "Gimme all your money or I won't let you by."

"I don't have any money," said George.

"Then gimme your lunch."

"You call this a lunch?" yelled Big Mike. "You'd better have something better than this tomorrow! Now get out of here."

George ran faster than he ever had before.

That day George had nothing to eat for lunch.
"Forget your lunch?" said Harriet. "Here,
you can have half of my peanut butter sandwich."

After school George raced home. He was afraid Big Mike would be waiting for him.

That night he ate an enormous dinner.

"Goodness, you're hungry this evening," said George's mother.

"Maybe you'd better pack me a bigger lunch tomorrow?" said George.

The next morning Big Mike took George's lunch again.

"Listen, Big Ears," he said, "you'd better have more cookies tomorrow."

That day George had nothing to eat for lunch again.

"Golly, George, I already ate my sandwich," said Harriet. "You're sure getting forgetful."

The next morning George sneaked some extra cookies into his lunch box. Then he took the long way to school, but Big Mike caught him anyway.

"Don't get tricky with me, Twitch Nose," said Big Mike as he grabbed George's lunch.

By the end of the week George was a nervous wreck. He couldn't pay attention in class, he jumped when anyone called his name, and he was hungry all the time.

"Something fishy is going on here," said Harriet on Friday. "You'd better tell me what it is, George."

So George told Harriet the whole story. He
felt a little better then, but not much.

"We should tell the principal," said Harriet.
"It won't do any good," said George. "Big
Mike doesn't go to this school."

"Hmmm," said Harriet. "I think I have an
idea. Meet me at my house tomorrow morning."

Saturday morning George biked over to Harriet's. He shook all the way there.

"Here's the plan," said Harriet, and she whispered into George's ear as she pulled him into the kitchen.

The two of them set to work making a lunch. First they made two tunafish sandwiches. They poured half a jar of garlic powder into the tunafish.

Then they filled a thermos halfway with
vegetable soup. They filled it the rest of the
way with vinegar.

Then they mixed hot pepper into some fruit
cocktail and put it in a jar.

Finally they separated some cream-filled cookies. They ate the frosting, then filled the cookies with lard instead.

Then they went to see Harriet's cousin, Lance.

On Monday morning George hid his real lunch in his school bag and carried the lunch he and Harriet had made. Then he set off for school. Lance followed close behind but kept out of sight.

Sure enough, Big Mike stole George's lunch again.

"Won't he be surprised," said George. "I sure taught that Big Mike a lesson!"

But just to be on the safe side, George had Lance follow him to school for the rest of the week.